I0820240

Misty Copeland, Katherine Johnson, and Mae Jemison!

CONTENTS

Ready-to-Read

SIMON SPOTLIGHT
An imprint of Simon & Schuster Children's Publishing Division
New York London Toronto Sydney New Delhi
1230 Avenue of the Americas, New York, New York 10020
This Simon Spotlight edition December 2024

Simon & Schuster: Celebrating 100 Years of Publishing in 2024
For information about special discounts for bulk purchases, please contact
Simon & Schuster Special Sales at 1-866-506-1949 or business@simonandschuster.com.
Manufactured in China 0824 SCP
2 4 6 8 10 9 7 5 3 1
These books have been previously cataloged with the Library of Congress.
ISBN 978-1-6659-6572-9
ISBN 978-1-4814-7045-2 (*Misty Copeland* ebook)
ISBN 978-1-5344-0342-0 (*Katherine Johnson* ebook)
ISBN 978-1-4814-7651-5 (*Mae Jemison* ebook)
These titles were previously published individually by Simon Spotlight.

YOU
SHOULD
MEET
Misty
Copeland

Misty Copeland

CONTENTS

Introduction

Have you ever dreamed of being a ballerina? Have you wondered about the hard work that goes into twirling across a stage, or flying through the air in a giant leap? What if you looked different from all the ballerinas you'd ever seen, but you knew in your heart you should be one?

If you've ever wondered about those things, then you should meet Misty Copeland. Misty is the first African American woman to earn the position of principal dancer, the highest level a dancer can achieve, in the American Ballet Theatre. She has also inspired young people all over the world to go after their **dreams**.

Welcome
to
Californi

Chapter 1
Before Ballet

Misty was born on September 10, 1982, in Kansas City, Missouri. She had three older siblings, two brothers and a sister. When Misty was two, her mother left her father. The family took a bus across the United States to San Pedro, California. Misty wouldn't see her father again until she was grown up.

From then on, Misty was on the move. Her mother married and divorced two more times and had two more children. Each time her mother divorced, the family moved to a new house.

Misty enjoyed being part of a big family, but all the changes made her feel worried. She worried most about making mistakes at school. She made up for that by getting to school an hour early every morning. She studied and got good grades.

Life wasn't all school, though. Misty loved to watch gymnastics on television. She taught herself to do cartwheels, backbends, and other moves.

Dancing around the house to Mariah Carey's music videos also made Misty happy. When she was in middle school, she *choreographed* a dance (that means she created a sequence of steps and moves) for herself and her two best friends. They danced in the school talent show.

Misty loved being onstage. "I felt fierce," she later wrote in her autobiography.

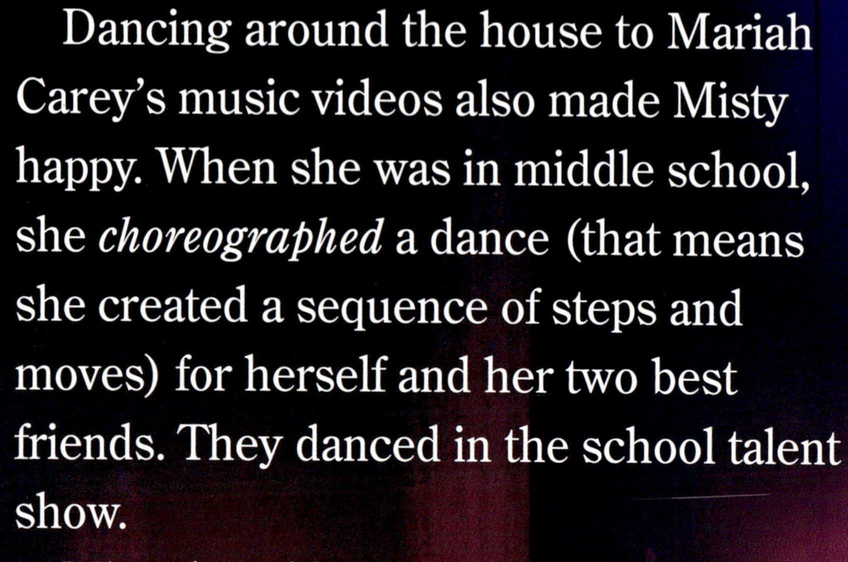

SCORE
HOME
VISITOR

Chapter 2
First Steps

Middle school brought Misty new challenges. She decided to try to win a place on the school's *drill team* like her sister, Erica, had done before her. A drill team performs dance moves for a school audience. Misty wanted to be more than just part of the team. She wanted to be the captain.

Misty created her own routine and danced her best. One night she got a phone call from the team's coach, Elizabeth Cantine. Misty was named captain of the drill team! She loved being team captain. Practice was one place where she didn't feel worried.

Coach Cantine had a background in ballet. She taught Misty some ballet moves for the drill team and saw how good Misty was. She gave Misty the idea of taking a ballet class at the local Boys & Girls Club.

The Boys & Girls Club was another place where Misty didn't feel worried. The Boys & Girls Club is a safe place where kids can go after school to play sports, be creative, and have fun. Misty and her brothers and sisters went to the local club almost every day after school.

Misty wanted to make her coach happy. Even though she knew nothing about ballet, she went to the class. She didn't have a leotard or tights or ballet shoes. For two weeks Misty sat and watched the ballet dancers. She was afraid she would look silly if she tried to dance. But one day she did try, wearing her gym clothes and dancing in her socks.

Most serious ballerinas start dancing by the time they are seven years old. Misty was thirteen when she started. Her ballet teacher, Cindy Bradley, saw Misty's talent from the very beginning. She knew right away that Misty was a special dancer. It wasn't long before Misty left the Boys & Girls Club to dance every day in Cindy's ballet studio.

Chapter 3
Becoming a Ballerina

Soon Misty started to feel like a ballerina. She took classes with dancers who had been training for years, and kept up with them. Within a few months she was dancing *en pointe*, or on the tips of her toes. It takes most dancers years to develop this skill. In just a few months Misty was dancing difficult steps and soaring past the other dancers.

At the same time, things were not good at home. Misty's second stepfather often said hurtful things to her mother and to her siblings. The family left him and moved into a small motel room next to a busy highway.

Misty got a ride to the ballet studio with Cindy after school every day, but she had to take a long bus ride home. By then ballet was more than a hobby for Misty. The world of ballet was a place where she felt safe and happy, a place where she was able to shine. The ballet classes were worth the hour-long bus ride home every night.

Misty's mother saw how hard her daughter worked. She saw how tired Misty was. She told Misty it was too much, she'd have to give up ballet. Misty was heartbroken. The next day she cried as she told Cindy she couldn't come back to class.

Cindy told Misty's mother that Misty had a chance to be a star. Cindy didn't want Misty to leave class. Together Cindy and Misty's mother decided that Misty would live with Cindy during the week to be closer to school and at the motel with her family on weekends.

Misty's weekends were often busy with performances. She spent less and less time with her family. After almost three years Misty's mother told Misty that it was time to come home.

Both Misty's mother and Cindy thought they knew what was best for Misty. Misty's mother wanted her to move back home. Cindy wanted Misty to continue to live with her and to dance. The two women went to court and asked the court to decide where Misty should live. Misty was scared and sad. She wanted to make everyone happy.

AMERICAN
BALLET
THEATRE
Misty

Chapter 4
Misty Takes New York by Storm

The court decided that Misty would move back in with her family and take lessons at a new studio closer to home after school. After a few months her mother got a better job and they moved out of the motel. Misty soon settled into her new ballet studio, even though she missed her old friends and teachers.

Misty continued to learn in her new studio. The following year she was invited to a summer program at the American Ballet Theatre (ABT) in New York City. ABT is one of the best ballet companies in the world.

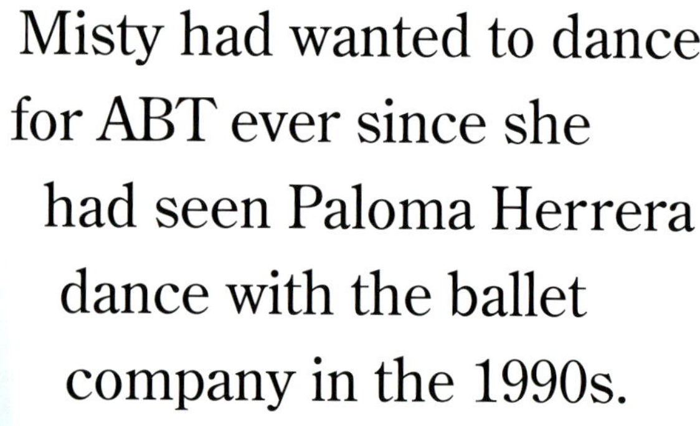

Misty had wanted to dance for ABT ever since she had seen Paloma Herrera dance with the ballet company in the 1990s. Paloma was one of the youngest stars in the history of ABT. She was fifteen when she moved from Argentina to New York to join the *corps de ballet*, the group of dancers in the background of ballet performances. Two years later she was promoted to soloist. When she was nineteen, Paloma became a principal dancer.

Misty knew that she had started dancing too late to become a principal dancer at nineteen, but she wanted to follow Paloma's path. If she made it to Paloma's level, she would be the first

African American woman to do so in the history of the American Ballet Theatre.

Now Misty was going to dance for the same ballet company in New York City. “I was ready to take the Big Apple by storm,” Misty wrote in her autobiography. And she did. After she completed the summer program, ABT invited her to join them full-time.

It was a hard decision, but Misty decided to go home and finish her last year of high school. She hoped that ABT would make her the same offer the

following summer. And they did.

Misty became a member of the corps de ballet. She was the only African American woman out of eighty dancers. She worried that she would never fit in.

The days were long and hard. Misty took a ninety-minute ballet class every morning and then rehearsed for seven hours.

At night the dancers performed.

By the end of her first year, Misty was beginning to work her way up in the company. Then one day while she was dancing, pain exploded in her back. The stress of dancing had injured a bone in Misty's spine. For the next year she wore a back brace for twenty-three hours a day and couldn't dance.

During that year Misty's body changed. She became curvier than she had been before. Once she was able to dance again, she had to learn how to dance all over again in her new body. People began to tell her that she was too "athletic" to be a

ballerina. Her strong muscles stood out.

No one said that there wasn't a place in ballet for an African American woman, but Misty knew some people thought that. She just kept dancing and showed them how **graceful and strong** she was.

Six years after she joined the corps de ballet, Misty was named a *soloist*. A soloist is a performer with a special role in the ballet. It had been over twenty years since an African American woman had had that honor at American Ballet Theatre. The first African American women soloists had been Nora Kimball and Shelley Washington, who had joined the company as soloists in the 1980s. Now Misty's name was being added to that short list.

Chapter 5
Twirling into History

It wasn't long before Misty was standing out because of her incredible dancing. People outside the ballet world noticed her too.

Misty starred in a commercial for a sportswear company. In the commercial a little girl read a letter listing all the reasons why she could never be a ballerina, such as having the wrong body type for ballet, and at age thirteen she was too old to be considered. As the girl spoke, Misty twirled and leapt across the stage. Within one week, more than four million people had watched the commercial on the Internet.

The support of Misty's friends and fans helped her to keep doing the hard work to win the best roles in the ballet company. In the spring of 2012 Misty was picked for the lead role in *The Firebird*, a famous ballet. Misty was the first African American woman ever to dance the role for a major ballet company, and she earned rave reviews. But dancing had also caused another injury. Misty needed surgery to repair fractures in her leg.

Some doctors said she would never dance again. But Misty didn't give up. She worked hard and got better, and danced more roles, including the lead role in *Swan Lake*. The lead in *Swan Lake* is the role every ballerina imagines herself performing. Dancing this role was a dream come true.

Misty also wrote her autobiography and a separate picture book called *Firebird*

Misty twirled into history on June 30, 2015, when her biggest dream came true. She was named a principal dancer for American Ballet Theatre. That's the highest level a ballerina can achieve. Principal dancers almost always get the biggest roles in ballet. Their pictures are also published in the ballet programs, and young dancers all over the world look up to them. Misty is the first African American woman to be a principal dancer in ABT's history.

What's next for this unstoppable ballerina? Only time will tell, but it's clear that Misty will continue to inspire young people to go after their dreams. A few days after being named principal dancer, she said, "You can dream big, and it doesn't matter what you look like, where you come from, what your background is. That's the example that I want to set and what I want to leave behind."

Now that you've met Misty Copeland, wouldn't you agree that anything is possible?

Dream big!

BUT WAIT . . .

THERE'S MORE!

Turn the page to learn more about ballet.

Learn the finer *pointes* of the five basic positions!

Lesson number one for any ballet dancer is how to hold their arms and legs. Sounds easy, right? There are five basic positions, and all of them take years of practice to get just right. If you try these positions at home, be careful and don't attempt to force your toes to turn all the way out to the side! It takes dancers many years of training to get their hips turned out enough that their toes point to the side. You can injure yourself if you try to force your legs into an unnatural position.

1

In **first position** the dancer's heels are together and their toes are pointed outward. This outward positioning of the feet is called *turn-out*. When a dancer first begins learning ballet, their feet will form a V in first position. As they slowly progress, the opening of the V will widen until their feet form a straight line. It takes many years of training to safely achieve a 180-degree turn-out. In first position the arms are held in front of the dancer, either an inch or two from the thighs or out in front of the stomach. The fingers should almost touch, and the arms should be rounded, as if the dancer were holding a beach ball.

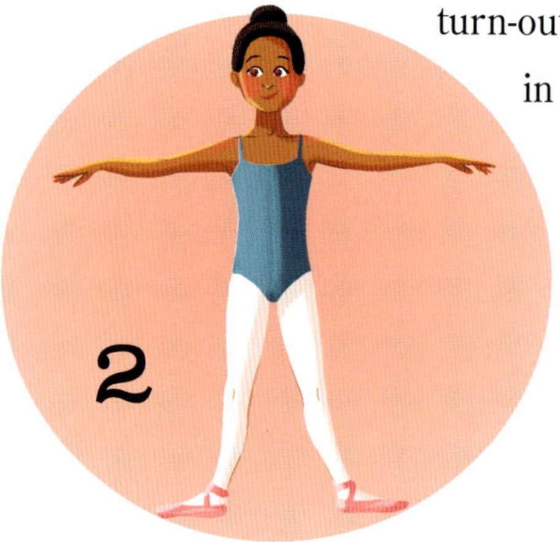

2

In **second position** the dancer's

heels are a few inches apart, and their toes are pointed outward. The arms are still slightly rounded but are held out to the sides.

In **third position** one foot is in front of the other. The heel of the front foot touches the arch, or middle of the back foot. The toes are pointed outward. One arm is raised above the head. The other arm is held out to the side. Third position for the feet is rarely used because it's so similar to fifth position, but third position for the arms is used regularly.

In **fourth position** one foot is a few inches in front of the other, and the toes are pointed outward. If the right foot is in front, the right arm is raised above the head and the left is held out in front.

In **fifth position** the feet are arranged the same as they are in third position, except the front foot covers the whole back foot. Both arms are slightly rounded and held above the head, with the fingers almost touching.

The History of Ballet

Ballet began as a party activity in fifteenth-century Italy, during the *Renaissance* (say: REN-nah-sance), a time when people in Europe were very interested in art and literature. The nobility and court wore fancy masks and danced for their guests. The steps were arranged by a dancing master.

Settings, costumes, and even poetry were added to ballet performances in sixteenth-century France with *ballet de cour* (court ballet). The dancers wore masks and long ball gowns, and the way they moved was very different from how modern-day ballerinas move.

King Louis XIV was the first to hire professional ballet dancers. He was a fan of the pastime and played many roles himself. When he couldn't dance anymore, he paid the best performers to entertain him. Suddenly, ballet became a career.

King Louis XIV

In the mid-1700s Jean-Georges Noverre had the idea to tell a story through movement, the way an opera told a story through song. He created *ballet d'action*, and the art form took to the stage.

In the mid-nineteenth century, ballets such as *Giselle* called for gently floating spirits and fairies. To create this illusion, ballerinas wore flowing skirts and skimmed the floor in newly invented pointe shoes.

The second half of the nineteenth century brought us *The Nutcracker*, *The Sleeping Beauty*, and *Swan Lake*. Ballerinas' flowing skirts became short tutus, and dancers showed off complex pointe work, high leg lifts, and the elegant movements we see today.

Ballet has continued to grow and change. George Balanchine's (say: bal-an-SHEEN) ballets expressed ideas without telling stories. Martha Graham pioneered modern dance. Alvin Ailey helped popularize modern dance and brought African American culture into the spotlight on ballet's biggest stages.

In addition to those we've mentioned, we can thank countless individuals for transforming ballet from a Renaissance pastime into a celebrated and soaring art.

Ballet by the Numbers

- Ballet dancers who aspire to dance professionally take up to 15 classes per week and usually begin training when they are 7 years old.

- A professional dancer (someone who earns a living by dancing) usually retires when he or she is 30 to 40 years old.

- An average professional ballerina can go through 6 pairs of pointe shoes a week and 1 pair per performance.

- A pair of pointe shoes costs about $50 to $80.

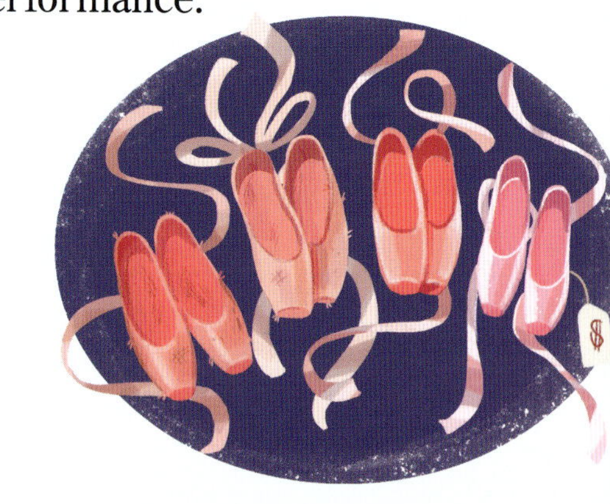

• The average ballerina trains for 8 to 10 years before becoming a professional.

• The average professional ballet dancer is practicing, rehearsing, and performing for 7 to 10 hours each day.

• American Ballet Theatre employed 18 principals, 13 soloists, and 57 corps de ballet dancers as of September 2015.

• In addition to the 5 basic positions, ballet dancers must learn the 8 positions of the body used in performances.

• One of the most famous ballet choreographers, George Balanchine, created 465 works in his lifetime.

Now that you've met Misty, what have you learned?

1. In what year was Misty born?

a. 1932 b. 1952 c. 1982

2. Misty's life has been "on the move" since she was two years old. What does that mean?

a. She has experienced many changes since then.

b. She started taking ballet lessons when she was two years old.

c. Since she learned to walk, she's had a hard time sitting still.

3. For how long did Misty train before she was dancing en pointe, or on the tips of her toes?

a. A few days b. A few months c. A year

4. When did Misty realize she wanted to dance for American Ballet Theatre?

a. When she moved to New York b. When she saw Paloma Herrera perform

c. During her first ballet class

5. What did Misty mean when she said she was ready to "take the Big Apple by storm?"

a. She wanted to become a star in New York City.

b. She wanted to tour San Francisco as quickly as possible.

c. She wanted to fly over Manhattan.

6. When people said Misty was too "athletic" to be a ballerina, what did they mean?

a. She spent too much time at the gym instead of rehearsal.

b. She stood out because she was an awkward dancer.

c. She didn't look like a ballerina because her muscles stood out.

7. What was historical about Misty's being promoted to principal dancer at American Ballet Theatre?

a. She was the first African American dancer admitted to the company.

b. She was the first African American woman to be made principal dancer at the company.

c. She had the greatest number of injuries of any American Ballet Theatre principal dancer.

8. Misty says she wants to set an example. What is that example?

a. Practice makes perfect. b. A ballerina can achieve anything.

c. You can dream big no matter what your background is.

Answers: 1. c 2. a 3. b 4. b 5. a 6. c 7. b 8. c

Katherine Johnson

Katherine Johnson

CONTENTS

f(v)
= 1,230 + x²
Px[q]
VALUE
2
8
10
√2x² - 1 =
a(b/c)²
42, 43, 45°

Introduction

What is your favorite subject in school? Have you ever thought about why you like it so much? Have you ever wondered what kind of a career you might have someday that involves your favorite subject?

You should meet Katherine Johnson.

From the time she was a very little girl, Katherine loved math. And she knew why, too. “It was hard,” she said, remembering doing math in school, “but when you got it, you got it. You had to work for it. There was a right and a wrong, and you knew when you got there.”

Another thing Katherine knew was that she would someday find a job that involved math. But even she never imagined that her math skills would help the US put the first man on the moon!

Chapter 1
A Family to Count On

On August 26, 1918, Katherine Johnson was born in White Sulphur Springs, West Virginia. She was the youngest of four children. Her father owned a farm, and her mother had been a teacher.

Ever since she could remember, Katherine was interested in learning—about almost anything! She couldn't wait to be old enough to start elementary school. Before then, she followed her siblings to school and tried to go in with them!

Most of all, Katherine loved to count. She counted family members, dishes, the number of steps from home to school, and so much more. "Everything is math!" Katherine said.

Katherine believed she got her gift for numbers from her father.

Even though her father had only completed the sixth grade, Katherine said he was the smartest man she ever knew. "He could look at a tree and know how many boards of wood he could get out of it," she said. He could solve any math problem too.

Before she turned six, Katherine finally started school. Because she could already read, she skipped first grade. She would skip fifth grade too. In school Katherine always had her hand in the air to ask questions. Her teachers encouraged her.

Each night Katherine and her siblings did their homework seated around a big table. "After I finished mine, I'd help them with theirs!" she recalled.

When Katherine was a little girl, most African Americans did not go to school beyond eighth grade. They went to work to help their families. At the time, the country also had a history of racial segregation. That means that there were many separate things for African Americans and white Americans, including schools. Katherine's hometown did not even have a high school for African Americans.

Katherine's father, however, was determined that all of his children would go to high school and to college, too. When Katherine's eldest brother, Charles, was ready for high school, Katherine's father moved the entire family one hundred and twenty miles away to Institute, West Virginia.

Institute had a high school for African Americans, and Katherine's mother and father made sure all their children graduated from it.

Katherine's parents

Katherine, her siblings, and her mother spent each school year in the town of Institute. Katherine's father stayed in White Sulphur Springs to take care of the farm. Because Katherine had skipped two grades, she started high school when she was just ten. She became a college freshman at fifteen. Most people start college when they are around eighteen years old!

Chapter 2
Math, Katherine's Number One Love

Katherine found it very exciting to be a student at West Virginia State College. There seemed to be countless classes she wanted to take! She especially loved French and thought she wanted to graduate with a degree in French, but she still loved math, too!

Then one day she ran into Mrs. Lacey, a math teacher she knew from back home. Mrs. Lacey insisted that Katherine sign up for her class. Mrs. Lacey made Katherine realize she wanted to concentrate on her math skills and graduate with a degree in math.

"I was just as fascinated with college math as I had been with high school math," Katherine remembered. She decided to major in math *and* French!

Katherine took every single math class the college offered. One of her other math professors, W. W. Schieffelin Claytor, even created a couple of new classes just for her! He told Katherine, "You would make a good research mathematician."

Katherine asked him, "What does a research mathematician do?"

Mr. Claytor answered, "You do research in mathematics!" (**Research** means to study materials in order to confirm facts and research new conclusions.)

Katherine asked, "Well, where do you get a job doing that?"

His reply was, "That's going to be *your* problem. But I am going to have you ready!"

Katherine *was* ready by the time she graduated with honors in 1937 at the age of eighteen. It was difficult at this time, however, for many African Americans, especially women, to find good jobs. The only good jobs for college-educated African American women at the time were teaching or nursing jobs.

After a few months Katherine got her first job. She taught French and piano to elementary school children. At her father's urging she went to graduate school too. During this time Katherine also got married and started a family of her own.

In 1952 Katherine heard that the National Advisory Committee for Aeronautics (NACA), a government agency in Newport News, Virginia, was hiring African American female research mathematicians! Within a week she and her family moved to Newport News.

Katherine immediately applied for a job at NACA. She found out that all the jobs for the coming year had already been filled. So Katherine became a substitute teacher and did other work too. Then, the following year, NACA offered her a job!

Katherine was thrilled. She was finally going to find out what a research mathematician did.

Chapter 3
A "Computer" in a Skirt

Katherine started at NACA in June 1953. The agency was dedicated to flight research. Among other things, NACA engineers had developed the first aircraft that could fly faster than the speed of sound.

NACA's research work required a lot of complex math. In 1953, electronic computers were not generally used, so research mathematicians, who were often called "computers," did the math that the engineers needed.

Katherine joined a group of about twelve African American women who were research mathematicians. There was also a group of white American women research mathematicians. The two groups worked and ate separately until the Civil Rights Movement that had started in the 1950s brought an end to racial segregation in 1964.

At NACA, Katherine was finally able to see firsthand what a research mathematician did—and she loved it! "You had big data sheets, with maybe fifteen or twenty columns across and twenty-five lines down," she explained, "and you solved those all the way across for days. It was fascinating!"

Research mathematicians sometimes left the group and worked full-time with engineers on a specific project. When the project was done, they returned to the group. Shortly after she arrived, Katherine was sent to work full-time on a flight research project. The engineers quickly became impressed by Katherine's math skills, as well as her interest in learning as much about the project as she could.

Working on the project, Katherine did what she always did: She asked a lot of questions! She knew that the more she understood about the project, the better her contribution to it would be.

"There is no such thing as a dumb question," Katherine always said. "It's dumb if you don't ask it." Because of her intelligence, curiosity, and upbeat attitude, Katherine never returned to the group of research mathematicans. She was requested on many special projects.

Katherine was a valued member of NACA when the agency turned its focus to space exploration in the late 1950s. The United States and the Soviet Union were then the two most powerful countries in the world. (The Soviet Union was a former federation of Communist republics occupying the northern half of Asia and part of Eastern Europe. Its capital and largest city was Moscow.) However, each wanted to be number one, and that included being the first nation to explore space. In 1958, NACA became the National Aeronautics and Space Administration, or NASA. Its efforts became devoted to what was called the "Space Race."

Little did Katherine know at the time just how far she, NASA, the US, and the entire world would go!

Chapter 4
Katherine Takes Off!

The Soviet Union took an early lead in the Space Race. In 1957 they launched *Sputnik 1*. It was the first man-made satellite to successfully orbit the Earth. (A **satellite** is a small object that revolves around a larger object.) The US launched its first satellite the following year.

The Soviet Union took the lead again when it came to sending a man into space. On April 12, 1961, cosmonaut Yuri Gargarin (a Russian astronaut is called a **cosmonaut**) orbited the Earth aboard *Vostok 1*. The US followed less than a month later. On May 5, 1961, astronaut Alan Shepard made a partial orbit around the Earth in *Freedom 7*.

It had required extremely complex and precise mathematical calculations to arrive at the proper flight path for the spacecraft and to keep Shepard safe. Who had done the math? Katherine!

For her entire career Katherine insisted that no one person was responsible for any specific achievement. She believed in teamwork. However, she also knew just how skilled she was at math. NASA knew it too!

NASA put Katherine on the team that worked to send *Friendship 7* and astronaut John Glenn into space on February 20, 1962. Katherine worked on the tracking system that would predict, within two miles, where the spacecraft would land after making three full orbits around the Earth.

Patch worn by *Friendship 7* astronauts

NASA was relying on its first electronic computer to calculate *Friendship 7*'s flight path. John Glenn, however, had more faith in Katherine than in any new technology. He insisted that Katherine check the computer's numbers! He said, "If she says the computer is right, I'll take it."

Katherine worked for a day and a half on the calculations that the computer had done. She arrived at the same exact numbers!

Katherine's precise spaceflight calculations were not her only unique accomplishments at NASA. Early in NASA's history, only men attended the briefing meetings where spaceflight was discussed. Katherine wanted to be at those meetings and kept asking if she could go. She even asked, "Is there a law against it?"

Katherine's persistence paid off. She was eventually invited to attend all briefing meetings, and she participated in the discussions. She was also the first woman in her division to have her name included on a report. The report contained theories Katherine had helped to develop about how to launch, track, and bring back spacecraft.

Katherine also became an important member of the team behind *Apollo 11*.

By the late 1960s both the Soviet Union and the US had landed unmanned vehicles on the moon, but neither had ever put a person on the moon. *Apollo 11* was going to be the first manned spaceflight to land on the moon.

On July 16, 1969, *Apollo 11* launched and headed to the moon with three astronauts on board. Katherine had computed the path to get them there. The landing and successful return of *Apollo 11*'s flight to the moon made headlines all around the world. And it could not have been possible without Katherine's help.

Four days later, on July 20, 1969, Katherine, along with the rest of the world, watched on television as astronaut Neil Armstrong took mankind's first step on the moon. The little girl from White Sulphur Springs who loved to count had helped the US make world history! The US was now the clear leader in the Space Race.

Katherine admitted to being concerned about the return flight. “If we were off by just a few feet or seconds, they were done for,” she remembered. “The astronauts wouldn’t be able to return home.”

Katherine had no need to worry. Her calculations were as accurate as ever. The astronauts splashed down safely in the Pacific Ocean on July 24, 1969.

Chapter 5
An Infinite Contribution

Katherine worked on every space mission at NASA until she retired in 1986. She had done extraordinary, history-making work while raising her family, dealing with the death of her first husband in 1956, and getting remarried in 1959. “I found what I was looking for at NASA,” said Katherine. “Never did I get up and say I don’t want to go to work.”

Katherine received many honors for her contribution to the US space program, including a flag that had gone to the moon. A building has also been named after her at NASA's Langley Research Center in Hampton, Virginia. In 2015 she received the Presidential Medal of Freedom. It is the highest honor an American civilian can receive. Katherine was ninety-seven at the time—an impressive number even for a math lover!

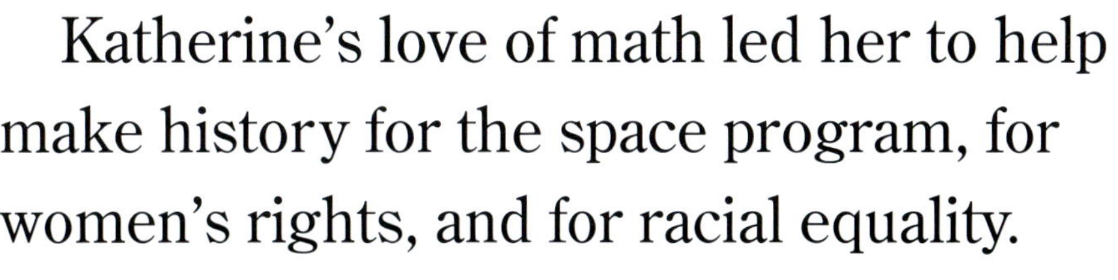

Katherine's love of math led her to help make history for the space program, for women's rights, and for racial equality. Through it all, Katherine remained humble about her remarkable achievements. She liked to quote her father, who used to tell her and her siblings, "You are as good as anybody. But you're no better."

Katherine shared her father's saying with the many students she spoke to after she retired. She wanted to encourage young people the way she had been encouraged. She also told them, "I like to learn. You can learn if you want to."

Katherine Johnson died on February 24, 2020, at the age of 101. Now that you've met Katherine Johnson, don't *you* want to learn as much about your favorite subject as you can? Katherine is proof that if you stay grounded in what you love, the places you go can be out of this world!

BUT WAIT . . .

THERE'S MORE!

Turn the page to learn how sailors use the stars to guide them, some facts about outer space, and some cool careers that use math.

Star Power!

Long before Katherine helped humans travel to outer space, outer space helped humans travel the earth.

In ancient times most cultures kept land in sight when they sailed. It was a very slow way to travel across the ocean, but it helped keep ships from getting lost.

Over one thousand years ago Arab people found a way to sail straight across the Indian Ocean from one port to another. They used the North Star!

The North Star is a bright star in the handle of the constellation called the Little Dipper.

The North Star is special because it does not move across the sky. But if you travel north, the star appears to be higher in the sky. If you travel south, it appears to be lower.

Try it! Look across the room at something high on the wall, like a clock. As you walk toward the clock, you have to look up higher and higher to keep the clock in sight. The clock appears to be higher, just like the North Star.

To navigate, the Arab people created a tool called a kamal. In Arabic, "kamal" means "guide." It was a simple tool made of a wooden rectangle and a string. The kamal measured the height of the North Star. That told the sailors how far north they were.

If sailors knew how far north a port was, they could sail across the ocean directly to it. They simply sailed north or south from their home port until the kamal told them they were in the right spot.

With their ability to cross oceans, the Arab people traveled faster and more safely. They were able to trade with other cultures, earn money, and expand their territory.

Math Makes It Work!

From bakers to website makers, everyone uses math. But if you love solving problems, these awesome careers will add up to a lot of fun!

Want to create?

Engineers use math and science to help make almost anything you can think of!

Civil engineers plan out parts of cities and towns, like bridges, buildings, and sewers.

Mechanical engineers design mechanical engines, like those in cars, tools, and even toys!

Electrical engineers have a hand in designing electrical systems—from the ones found in smartphones to the power plants that keep the lights on in cities and towns.

Chemical engineers work with substances. They can help figure out how to make food taste better or to make fabric softer.

Aerospace engineers think up things that fly, like planes and helicopters.

Astronautical engineers are behind anything bound for outer space, like space shuttles and satellites.

Software engineers build worlds inside of computers. That's everything from the calculator on a smartphone to video games and virtual reality!

Want to discover?

These careers use math to collect information and make predictions.

Astronomers find new planets, stars, and so much more by watching and charting the night sky.

Meteorologists predict the weather using satellites, radar, and lots of cool tools.

Sports statisticians crunch numbers to tell newscasters and fans when a record has been set or an unlikely achievement has been made.

Music data journalists figure out which songs are popular, who might like which artists, and even what the next big hit will sound like.

These are just a few of the many jobs for people who love math!

Outer Space by the Numbers

- Our solar system has 1 star, 8 planets, 173 moons, and more than 3,400 comets and 715,000 asteroids. These numbers often change as we explore and make discoveries.

- The Earth's moon is about 238,855 miles away, or the length of 30 Earths sitting side by side.

- In our galaxy, the Milky Way, astronomers think there are between 100 and 400 billion stars, or maybe even more!

- *Voyager 1* became the 1st man-made object to leave our solar system.

• *Voyager 1* and *2* launched in 1977 and had enough power to send information back to Earth until 2020—that's 43 years!

• Mars is, on average, 140 million miles from Earth.

• The temperature in outer space is -455 degrees Fahrenheit. That's more than 300 degrees colder than the coldest place on Earth, the South Pole!

• *Curiosity*, NASA's Mars rover, arrived on August 5, 2012, on Mars after a journey of 8 months. It is studying the planet's environment to find out if life is possible on Mars.

Now that you've met Katherine, what have you learned?

1. What did Katherine's father own?

a. farm | b. bank | c. store

2. When Katherine was little, what did most African American girls do after eighth grade?

a. go to ninth grade | b. learned to drive | c. help their families

3. What was Katherine's first job?

a. research mathematician | b. French teacher and piano teacher | c. physicist

4. What country did the US compete with in the "Space Race"?

a. the Soviet Union | b. Canada | c. France

5. What did Katherine do for *Freedom 7*?

a. trained the astronauts | b. calculated the flight path | c. designed the rockets

6. What did Katherine help NASA achieve?

a. mankind's first step on the moon | b. the first American orbiting earth | c. both

7. Before Katherine, how many women had been allowed to attend NASA briefing meetings?

a. none | b. one | c. ten

8. What did Katherine work on until 1986?

a. every NASA space mission before she retired | b. *Apollo 11* | c. Sputnik

9. Every morning before she retired, Katherine wanted to do what?

a. quit her job | b. earn recognition | c. go to work

10. According to Katherine, you can learn if what?

a. you're lucky | b. you want to | c. you know how

Answers: 1.a 2.c 3.b 4.a 5.b 6.c 7.a 8.a 9.c 10.b

YOU
SHOULD
MEET
Mae
Jemison

Mae Jemison

CONTENTS

MAE JEMISON
NASA

Introduction

Have you ever looked up at the stars and wanted to fly? Have you dreamed of being an astronaut and blasting off into space? Or of being a dancer? Or being a doctor who brings medical care to people around the world?

If you've ever dreamed of any of those things, then you should meet Mae Jemison!

Mae is the first African American woman to become an astronaut. But she's much more than that. Mae is also . . .

a **scientist**

and **a dancer.**

And she's **a doctor, an author,**

and **a teacher.**

Today she's working to find ways for humans to travel beyond our solar system. Mae followed her dreams . . . all of them. Once you meet her, you'll know you can follow yours too!

Chapter 1
Early Dreams

Mae was born in Decatur, Alabama, on October 17, 1956. She has two older siblings, a sister and a brother. Her father was a carpenter and her mother taught elementary school.

When Mae was three years old, her family moved from Alabama to Chicago, Illinois. She thinks of Chicago as her hometown.

Mae always loved science. When her kindergarten teacher asked her what she wanted to be when she grew up, Mae said, “a scientist.” Many people at the time didn’t think it was possible for an African American girl to become a scientist. Women were more likely to become teachers and nurses than scientists.

“Don’t you mean a nurse?” the teacher asked.

“No, I mean a **scientist**,” Mae answered.

Other teachers tried to discourage Mae too. She wouldn't let them. She never stopped believing in herself. She stood strong in the face of other people's questions.

At home Mae was encouraged to be anything she wanted to be. "My parents were the best scientists I knew, because they were always asking questions," she said when she was grown up.

Mae considered herself a "busybody" and liked to get involved with her sister's and brother's science projects.

Once, she got a splinter in her thumb. Soon there was pus. Other kids might have been grossed out and just wanted it to go away, but not Mae. Mae wanted to know exactly what the pus was and where it came from. So she did a scientific study of pus to learn about how it fights infection to help our bodies heal.

Mae's family talked about many things around the dinner table, including the civil rights movement. The civil rights movement was a mass popular movement to secure equal access to and opportunities for the basic privileges and rights of US citizenship for African Americans. There were sometimes riots, and one time, National Guard soldiers came to Chicago to keep the peace. Mae was scared, but she promised herself that she wouldn't let fear keep her from doing what she wanted in the world.

The library was a place where Mae learned about science. She read all kinds of science books, especially ones about the stars.

Mae also followed the National Aeronautics and Space Administration's (NASA) space programs in the newspapers. She knew all about the astronauts and their missions.

"Growing up, I always assumed I would go into space," Mae said when she was older. "I remember being really, really irritated that there were no women astronauts."

Mae was inspired by the character Uhura, a female officer on the television show *Star Trek*. Uhura was played by the actress Nichelle Nichols. Eventually Mae got to meet Nichelle.

Mae believes that the best scientists are not only logical but creative too. She took all kinds of dance lessons growing up—ballet, jazz, modern, African, and even Japanese dancing. She wanted to be a professional dancer. She also designed and made clothes for her dolls, acted in school plays, and took art classes.

But science was always Mae's first love. She graduated high school at sixteen and won a scholarship to Stanford University to study engineering.

BSU

Chapter 2
Dreams on Earth

At Stanford University in California, Mae majored in chemical engineering. Biochemical engineering was her focus. A biochemical engineer creates things to make medical care better. Mae also majored in African and Afro-American history. And just like she had when she was younger, Mae combined art and creativity with science.

Mae created dance routines, acted in plays, and was president of the Black Student Union. She also learned to speak Swahili, an African language.

In college Mae decided that she wanted to be a medical doctor. When she graduated from Stanford, she moved to New York City to go to Cornell University Medical College. Mae studied hard, but she also made time for fun. She took dance lessons, and she went to the theater with friends.

During her summer breaks, Mae traveled to Kenya and Cuba to learn about medical care in other countries, especially for poor people.

She also worked in Thailand at a camp for *refugees*—people who had been driven away from their homes by war.

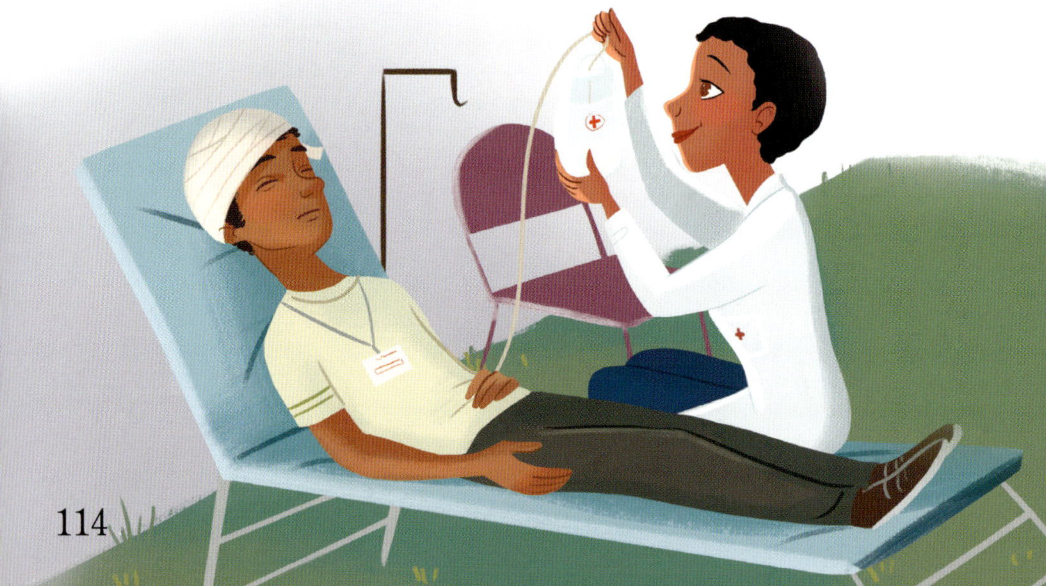

At first, Mae didn't want to be the kind of doctor who sees patients. She wanted to be the kind of doctor who does research. But working in other countries made her interested in bringing medicine to people in poor areas around the world.

After she became a doctor, Mae volunteered for the Peace Corps.

The Peace Corps is made up of Americans who bring things such as medical care, clean water, and education to people in underdeveloped countries. As a doctor for the Peace Corps, Mae went to Sierra Leone and Liberia, two countries in West Africa.

After two and a half years in Africa, Mae returned to California to work as a doctor. It was then that she remembered an early dream—a dream to fly into space.

She learned that NASA was accepting applications for the astronaut program, so Mae applied.

People who want to be astronauts must have college degrees in science, math, or engineering. They also need to have work experience in their fields and show NASA that they can be leaders.

Mae's application stood out. NASA asked her to travel to the Johnson Space Center in Houston, Texas, for interviews and physical tests. Mae must have shown them how smart and strong she was, because in June 1987 NASA asked her to be an astronaut candidate. She was one of fifteen chosen out of a group of two thousand people.

Mae's early dream was coming true. She was on her way to becoming an astronaut!

CONGRATULATIONS!
congratulat
MAE!

Chapter 3
Dreams about Space

Mae was chosen by NASA in 1987, but she wasn't an astronaut yet. She was an "astronaut *candidate*." A candidate is someone who is applying for a particular job. Astronaut candidates have to take classes and work hard to learn new things before they are given the title "astronaut."

One thing Mae had to learn before she could go into space was what it was like to be weightless. Astronauts call this *microgravity*. Gravity is the force that keeps humans—and everything else—from floating off Earth and into space. But in space you feel only a tiny amount of gravity's pull.

Astronauts need to be able to do their jobs while they are weightless. One way they learn how to do that is by flying in a special airplane. The plane makes many people sick to their stomachs.

The plane's nickname is the Vomit Comet!

Mae also needed to learn how to survive in the wilderness and in the water. That was in case her spaceship landed in the wrong place when it came back to Earth.

After a year of hard training, Mae was finally named an astronaut!

Not all astronauts fly into space. Many work on Earth, helping the astronauts who are in space. At first Mae worked as

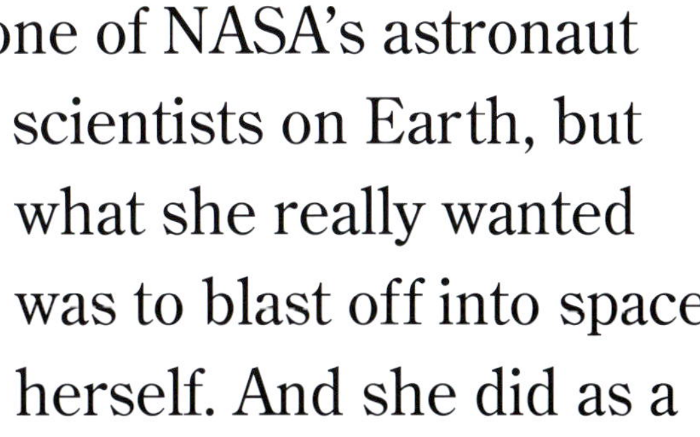

one of NASA's astronaut scientists on Earth, but what she really wanted was to blast off into space herself. And she did as a

Science Mission Specialist.

Science mission specialists perform experiments, among many other jobs, in space.

Chapter 4
Space!

On September 12, 1992, Mae became the first African American woman to travel into space.

The first white American woman to fly into space, Sally Ride, had done so in June 1983. The first African American male astronaut, Guion Bluford, had gone into space two months later in August 1983. Now Mae was making history by being both a woman and an African American.

Mae flew on the space shuttle *Endeavour*. She spent about eight days in space and completed almost 127 orbits of the Earth. In that time she traveled more than three million miles!

Mae wanted to celebrate art and creativity in space. Among other items, she brought a poster of an African American dancer and a statue made by a women's group in West Africa onto the shuttle.

In orbit, the astronauts did experiments. Mae wanted to know why some people get sick to their stomachs in space and how to make them feel better.

Mae also wanted to learn about how tadpoles grew when they were weightless. Mae discovered tadpoles grew just like they do in Earth's gravity.

"When we got back to Earth, the tadpoles were right on track," Mae told a reporter after her mission. The tadpoles later turned into frogs, just like they were supposed to.

Mae was never afraid in space. "I was very excited and happy," she said. She remembered being a young girl who loved to stare up at the stars.

"The first thing I saw from space was Chicago, my hometown. . . . Looking out the window of that space shuttle, I thought if that little girl growing up in Chicago could see her older self now, she would have a huge grin on her face."

The flight made Mae famous. She realized she could use her fame to talk about how important it is to take care of the planet. She also wanted people of all races to know they could be part of the scientific world.

Chapter 5
Life after Space

After flying into space, Mae decided to leave NASA and do other things. She became a college professor. She started a company that brings technology and better medical care to people in poor countries. She also became an actress when she appeared on the TV show *Star Trek: The Next Generation. Star Trek* was one of Mae's favorite TV shows when she was young.

Getting kids involved in science was also something Mae wanted to do. She started a camp for students who want to become scientists. The camp, called The Earth We Share, welcomes young scientists from all over the world.

These campers get to do more than hike or sleep in a tent. They use their imaginations and plan amazing things—such as a space mission to Mars!

The PERFECT HOME
THE EARTH
WE SHARE

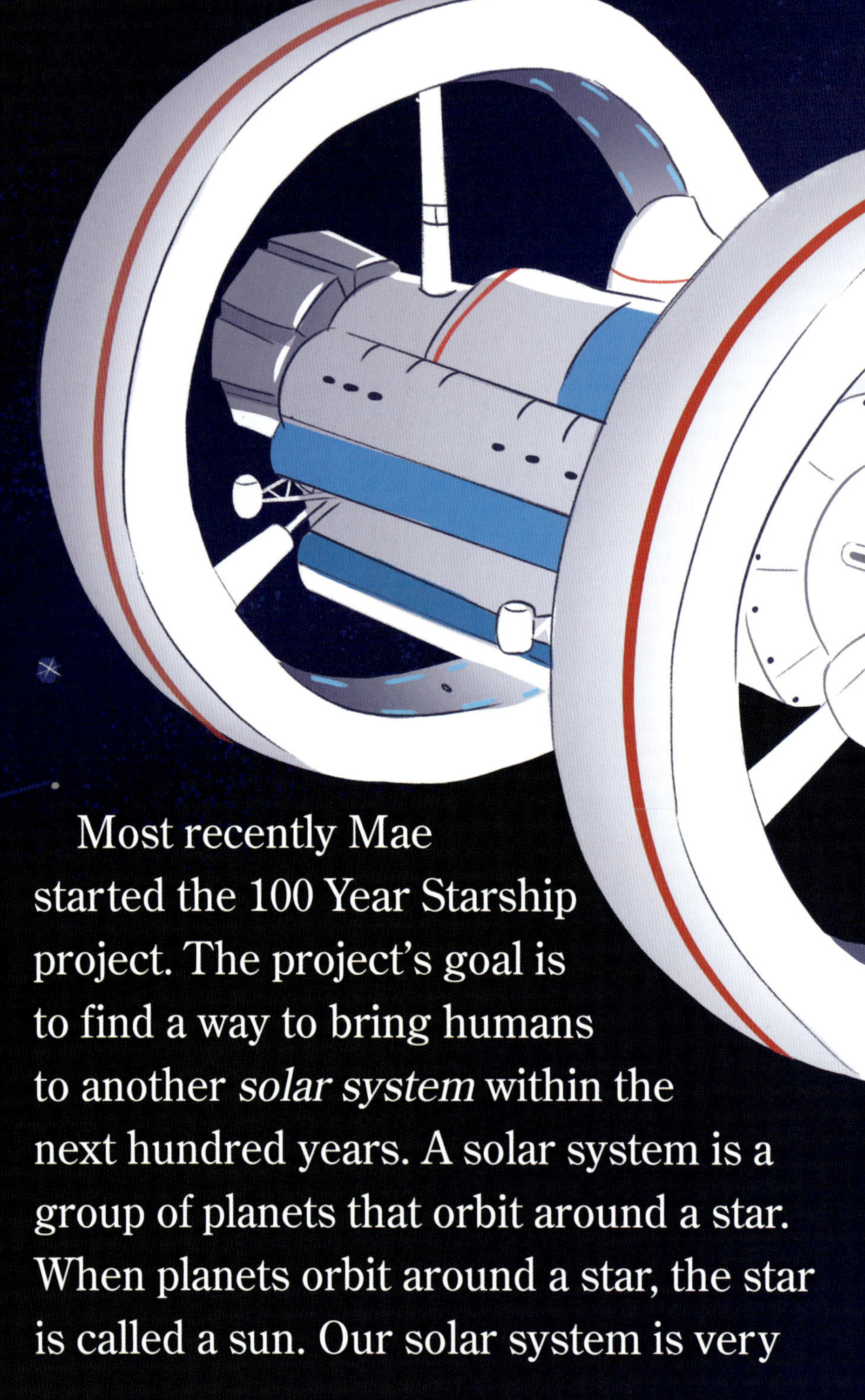

Most recently Mae started the 100 Year Starship project. The project's goal is to find a way to bring humans to another *solar system* within the next hundred years. A solar system is a group of planets that orbit around a star. When planets orbit around a star, the star is called a sun. Our solar system is very far away from any other solar system.

Today it would take us seventy thousand years to travel to another solar system!

The 100 Year Starship program will have to create everything from new kinds of energy to new kinds of filters that will keep air and water clean. A starship might need a garden for fresh fruits and vegetables, and things to help the astronauts survive on a new planet.

Most of all, Mae wants to make sure that all kinds of people, not just Americans and not just doctors, will have a chance to be involved.

Mae always believed in following her dreams, and she never let people tell her she couldn't. She also refused to become any one thing—a scientist or an artist, a doctor or a dancer. Mae believed she could do anything, and she did!

Now that you've met Mae Jemison, don't you think you can do the same thing? Reach for the stars—and more!

BUT WAIT . . .

THERE'S MORE!

Turn the page to try a science experiment similar to the ones Mae did in space, to read how Mae saved a life, and to read some facts about Mae's mission on board the space shuttle *Endeavour*.

Life Sciences Experiment

Aboard the space shuttle *Endeavour*, Mae did experiments to study how living things would react to being in space.

You can do experiments like Mae without even leaving your house! Follow the directions below to discover how plants react to three different environments.

Materials
3 plastic sandwich bags
12 dry pinto beans
3 paper towels
Water
Stapler with staples
Tape
Ruler
A journal or other place to write notes
A grown-up to help with the stapler

Step 1: Fold each paper towel into fourths so that it will fit into a sandwich bag.

Step 2: Put one folded paper towel into each bag.

Step 3: For each bag, staple four times through the paper towel, from right to left, about an inch from the bottom. Space out the staples evenly and make sure they are going straight across, not up and down.

Step 4: Inside the bag, place one bean on top of each staple.

Step 5: Find three different places to grow your beans, and tape one bag at each spot. Make sure each area has a different environment—someplace sunny, someplace shady, and someplace dark. Try taping one bag to a window, one to a wall beside a window, and another to the inside of a cabinet.

Step 6: Water your beans by pouring half an inch of water into each bag. Make sure the water doesn't rise above the staples.

Step 7: After about five days, you should see small green shoots sprouting from some of the beans.

Step 8: Keep watering your beans with half an inch of water once a week. Every time you water your plants, use the ruler to measure how long the shoots are, and then write down your findings. After a couple of weeks, you will start to notice a difference in the way the beans are growing.

Step 9: After two weeks, look at the measurements you've taken. Can you come to any conclusions about the way each environment affected the beans? Write your conclusions down.

Step 10: Now that you've made a discovery, share the results!

WHAT IT MEANS

This experiment studies how beans react to the amount of sunlight in their environment. You can study how beans react to other environments by changing the experiment. Make sure there is only one thing different about each environment for the beans. Otherwise, you won't know which change has affected the way they grow.

You can also experiment with:

- Different amounts of water.
- Different types of water, like salt water or sugar water.
- Different sources of light, like fluorescent or colored lightbulbs.
- Different temperatures.

Mae to the Rescue!

When Mae first became a doctor, she traveled to Sierra Leone in West Africa. She volunteered her medical services through the Peace Corps. Within two weeks one of the Peace Corps volunteers became very sick.

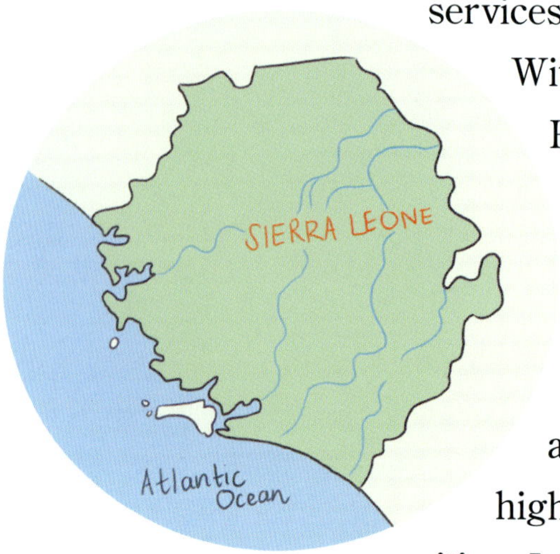

The other doctors thought the volunteer had malaria. Malaria is a disease that can cause a high fever, muscle pain, and vomiting. It is common in tropical climates like that of Sierra Leone. People can die of malaria if they are not treated. After receiving treatment for one day, the volunteer was worse. Mae knew that he did not have malaria. If he did not receive a different treatment, he would die.

Soon after the electricity went out at the hospital. Mae used a flashlight to search for medicine to give the volunteer a different treatment. Even if she found the medicine, it would not cure him completely. Mae was sure he was sick with meningitis. Meningitis is an illness that will kill a person if not treated correctly, and no one had the correct treatment nearby.

Mae ordered a military medical evacuation. That meant a plane would take the volunteer to an air force hospital for treatment. Mae was a new doctor, and she was giving an order that would cost more than eighty thousand dollars. The people at the US embassy did not think she could give such a big order.

Mae did not give up. She calmly explained that she had the power to give the order, and she clarified why it was absolutely necessary. She refused to take no for an answer—a man's life was at stake. The people at the embassy finally listened to her, and Mae evacuated with the volunteer. In all, she worked for fifty-six hours straight to save the man's life.

Thanks to Mae's self-confidence and brave decisions, the volunteer survived.

Mae's Mission by the Numbers

• Mae went into space on a mission called STS-47. It was the second flight of twenty-five for the space shuttle *Endeavour.*

• The mission lasted seven days, twenty-two hours, thirty minutes, twenty-three seconds from blast off to touchdown.

• The mission launched on September 12, 1992 at 10:23:00 a.m. Eastern Daylight Time and landed on September 20, 1992 at 8:53:23 a.m. Eastern Daylight Time.

• When the shuttle launched, it weighed 258,679 pounds. That's more than twenty-five school buses! When the shuttle landed, it weighed 218,854 pounds, having lost 39,825 pounds. Fuel, an external tank, and two solid rocket motors were either used up or ejected during the mission.

• The shuttle orbited Earth at an altitude, or height, of about 191 miles. That's about thirty-five times higher than the peak of Mount Everest.

• The shuttle orbited earth about 127 times, traveling 3.3 million miles. (That's close to the distance you'd travel to go to the moon and back seven times.)

• There were seven crew members.

• The STS-47 mission included three firsts: the first Japanese astronaut to fly aboard the shuttle, payload specialist Mamoru Mohri; the first African American woman to fly in space, mission specialist Mae Jemison; and the first married couple to fly on the same space expedition, mission specialists Mark C. Lee and N. Jan Davis.

Now that you've met Mae, what do you know about her?

1. What year was Mae born?
a. 1956 b. 1960 c. 1972

2. Mae believes that the best scientists are what?
a. Quiet b. Curious c. Stubborn

3. According to Mae, why were her parents the best scientists she knew?
a. They studied. b. They day dreamed. c. They asked questions.

4. Mae always knew she would do something specific. What was that?
a. Go to space b. Be a leader c. Study tadpoles

5. Besides science, what were some of Mae's interests?
a. Art and dance b. Geography and history c. Math and magic

6. When Mae finished medical school, what did she do next?
a. Started an organization b. Joined the Peace Corps c. Joined NASA

7. On September 12, 1992, Mae became the first ___ in space?
a. Woman b. Doctor c. African American woman

8. What did Mae do in space?
a. Conducted experiments b. Built robots c. Studied Earth

9. How did Mae feel in space?
a. Excited and afraid b. Sick but happy c. Excited and happy

10. After going to space, what did Mae want to do?
a. Help people and encourage space exploration.
b. Become a dancer and a writer. c. Go on a mission to the sun.

Answers: 1.a 2.b 3.c 4.a 5.a 6.b 7.c 8.a 9.c 10.a